This Little Tiger book belongs to:

_____

_____

_____

LITTLE TIGER PRESS

1 The Coda Centre, 189 Munster Road, London SW6 6AW
www.littletiger.co.uk • First published in Great Britain 2009
This edition published 2014 by Little Tiger Press, London
Text copyright © Paul Bright 2009 • Illustrations copyright © Lee Wildish 2009
Paul Bright and Lee Wildish have asserted their rights to be identified
as the author and illustrator of this work under the Copyright,
Designs and Patents Act, 1988
ISBN 978-1-84895-849-4
Printed in China • LTP/1900/0817/1013
2 4 6 8 10 9 7 5 3 1

For Katie, with love ~ P B

For Laura, Grace, and Oscar ~ L W

Paul
Bright

Lee
Wildish

CHARLIE'S SUPERHERO UNDERPANTS

SWAG

LITTLE TIGER PRESS

On a wild and windy day,
around about the end of May,
A great and gusting gale
blew the laundry clean away.

Socks and shirts, a woolly hat,
but much worse than all of that,
Young Charlie's Superhero Underpants.

POW!

As it soared into the sky,
the laundry billowed, flapped, and swirled,
Until it slowly scattered
to the corners of the world.

Though they searched
for days and nights,
with boats
and planes and satellites,

They found **no trace** of
Charlie's Underpants.

They had **POW!** across the front, in giant letters, bold and black,

With KERZAP! and OOF! and SPLAT! a little smaller on the back.

And villains would take fright
as Charlie pulled his pants up tight.
His Scarlet Superhero
Underpants.

Charlie packed
some sandwiches,
some sardines,
and some soap,

A mirror, fan and toothbrush,
and a big brass telescope.

"Don't worry and don't wait," he said,
"I may be back quite late.
But I've got to find my
Scarlet Underpants."

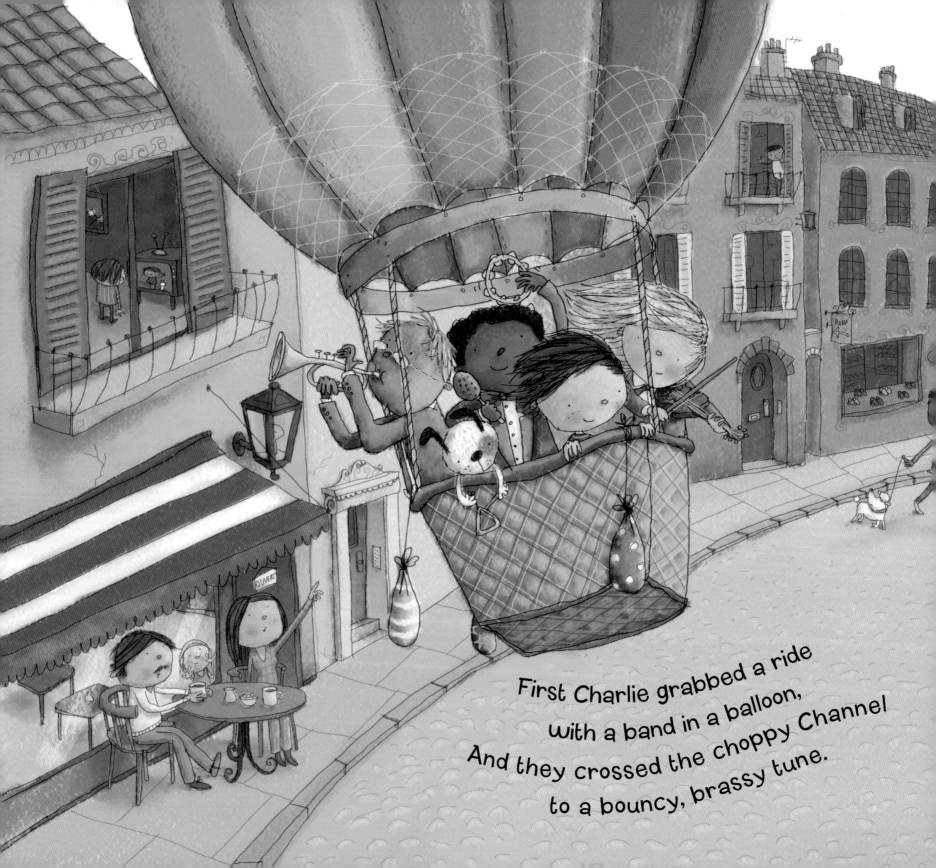

First Charlie grabbed a ride
with a band in a balloon,
And they crossed the choppy Channel
to a bouncy, brassy tune.

There they spied
a fine French fox,
wearing sister Sophie's socks,
But they saw no sign of Charlie's Underpants.

Angleterre

Culotte

Charlie hiked across
the endless plain of Serengeti,
Where the insects made him itchy
and the sunshine made him sweaty.

And there he saw a lion,
with a stripy shirt and tie on,
But no Scarlet Superhero Underpants.

Charlie climbed and clambered
up the plateau of Peru,
Where the breeze that blows at night
makes you shiver through and through,

And he found
a pair of llamas
wearing brother Ben's pajamas,

But he couldn't find his
Scarlet Underpants.

Charlie searched the length
of the mighty Mississippi,
Though the Mississippi's muddy
and the mud's all soft and slippy,

And an **alligator** sat,
wearing Grandpa's woolly hat,
But it wasn't wearing Charlie's Underpants.

Charlie was fed up.
He felt lonely, tired, and small,
On a steep and snowy hillside
in the mountains of Nepal.

When suddenly he saw,
in that land of ice and cold,
A huge and hairy creature,
something wondrous to behold.

Charlie blinked and rubbed his eyes.
It couldn't be . . .

it could . . .

For there, in Charlie's Underpants, a Yeti proudly stood.

"My underpants!" cried Charlie.
"They're the ones I love the most."

"But they're mine now," growled the Yeti.
"And they keep me warm as toast!"

"I'll swap you," Charlie said.
"You'll be snug from toes to head,
If you'll give me back my Scarlet Underpants."

Charlie thanked the Yeti
and he pulled his pants up tight.
They had POW! across the front,
so he'd put them on just right.

He raised one arm up high, and he flew into the sky . .

In his Scarlet Superhero

Underpants!